ANNA LIVIA PLU

CW00515084

JAMES JOYCE

Anna Livia Plurabelle

FABER & FABER

First published in 1930 in the Criterion Miscellany series
by Faber & Faber Ltd
Bloomsbury House, 74–77 Great Russell Street,
London WC1B 3DA
Second and third impressions 1930
Fourth impression 1932
Faber library edition 1997
This paperback edition published in 2017

Printed and bound by CPI Group (UK) Ltd, Croydon, CR0 4YY

All rights reserved
A Note on the Publishing History © Faber & Faber Ltd, 2017
Foreword © Edna O'Brien, 2017

The right of James Joyce to be identified as author of
this work has been asserted in accordance with Section
77 of the Copyright, Designs and Patents Act 1988

*This book is sold subject to the condition that it shall not,
by way of trade or otherwise, be lent, resold, hired out or
otherwise circulated without the publisher's prior consent
in any form of binding or cover other than that in which it
is published and without a similar condition including this
condition being imposed on the subsequent purchaser*

A CIP record for this book
is available from the British Library

ISBN 978-0-571-33371-4

FSC
www.fsc.org
MIX
Paper from
responsible sources
FSC® C020471

2 4 6 8 10 9 7 5 3 1

Foreword

In his fifties, as his genius escalated and transmogrified, Joyce admitted that he was at the end of English, saying he could no longer use ordinary words with daytime association, as this was a book of the night, 'bauchspeech from his innkempt house'. The Work in Progress, as it was called, would be *Finnegans Wake*, which took seventeen years in the doing. He wrote on the lid of a green suitcase that he had purchased in Bognor Regis, on a lacklustre honeymoon, wrote at night and laughed a lot at his own puns and polyglot language. His wife, Nora Barnacle, would get out of bed and tell him to stop writing and therefore stop laughing and moreover, the work was just chop suey. She was the one person who was not afraid of him and he loved her for it.

He had one-tenth vision and his list of ailments read like a footnote to the work – glaucoma, iritis, cataract, crystallised cataract, a nebula in the pupil, conjunctivitis, torn retina, blood accumulation and abscesses. He felt himself brother to Dean

Swift, 'whose glauque eyes glitt bedimmd to imm! whose fingrings creep o'er skull: til, qwench!' He wrote with thick coloured crayons and the help of three magnifying glasses. Sometimes his concentration was such that he almost lost consciousness and in extremis said, as he once did when writing *Ulysses*, that he was only 'a transparent leaf' away from madness. It is interesting that this tumble of language, this transubstantiation of word, these heavenly and unheavenly vocables, poured out from him without any thought of his blind eyes, as they came directly from the unconscious mind. It was when rereading and correcting that he became aware of impending wreckage. Yet he returned unremittingly to the task, wresting new, convoluted polyphonic words, building his Tower of Babel and fulfilling his prophecy of keeping the professors and the literati puzzled for hundreds of years.

Despite his antipathy towards and mockery of Freud, he now was invading the world of dream and he told the French journalist Edward Jaloux that his intention was 'to suit the aesthetic of the dream, where the forms prolong and multiply themselves, where the visions pass from the trivial to the apocalyptic, where the brain uses the roots of vocables to make others from them which will be capable of naming its phantasms, its allegories, its allusions.' At this point one is inclined, like Molly Bloom, to cry out, 'O rocks! . . . Tell us in plain words.'

As instalments of the work appeared in literary magazines, bile and condemnation proliferated. It was 'linguistic sodomy', the work of a shipwrecked mind and a monstrous leg-pull. Only Beckett saw Joyce's radical intention in grinding up words so as to extract their true purpose, then crossbreeding them and marrying sound with image to compose a completely new kind of language. Elsewhere, Joyce was assailed. D. H. Lawrence said that the instalments were all 'old fags and cabbage-stumps', Nabokov deemed them 'a cold pudding' and H. G. Wells warned Joyce that he had 'turned [his] back on common men', with the result being 'vast riddles', 'a dead end'. Ezra Pound, Joyce's most robust advocate, said that 'nothing short of divine vision or a new cure for the clap can possibly be worth all the circumambient peripherization'.

Joyce was all alone and discouraged. Was he 'an imbecile in my judgement of language'? he asked, then resolutely declared, 'I cannot go back.'

Even his faithful friend and patron Harriet Weaver Shaw began to have doubts about his puns, his aqueous passages and his riparian geography, fearing that he was losing touch with those readers astounded by the genius of *Ulysses*. He sought to allay her fears. He sent her keys to the more obscure words, but the keys were themselves mind-boggling. *Wolken* was 'a woollen cap of clouds' and *passencore* tallied with '*pas encore* and *ricorsi storici* of Vico'. His monthly income from her had to be doubled, because the harder he laboured the more he drank and tipped lavishly in restaurants. Then in October 1927 she received the following short note – 'I am working very hard on the final revise of Δ on which I am prepared to stake everything.' This was 'Anna Livia', his melodic chapter on which he hoped to win over recalcitrant readers. He wrote seven versions in all, constituting thousands of hours of labour, each episode more enriched, more exuberant and more transmutative. What he was doing was leaving a literary ghostmark for a world that was unprepared for it. Anna is both woman and river and 'her fluvial maids of honour', from all corners of the world, constitute three hundred and fifty river names. It appeared in *Criterion* magazine and at the instigation of T. S. Eliot, it was published by Faber & Faber for one shilling net. Joyce composed a ditty to boost sales:

Buy a book in brown paper
From Faber and Faber
To see Annie Liffey trip, tumble and caper.
Sevensinns in her singthings,
Plurabelle on her prose
Seashell ebb music wayriver she flows.

It begins in gay, effervescent mood, as two washerwomen on opposite sides of the River Liffey regale each other with scathing gossip. The sounds are of water, birdsong, bird cries, the beating of the battler on convent napkins, baby shawls, combies and sheets that a man and his bride embraced on. So they tuck up their sleeves, loosen the 'talk-tapes' and egg each other on to tell it 'in franca lingua. And call a spate a spate.' We are introduced to Anna, a shy, limber slip of a thing, 'in Lapsummer skirt and damazon cheeks', her hair down to her feet, 'her little mary' washed in bog water, with amulets of rhunerhinerstones around her neck. 'You'll die when you hear.' We learn of her nymphet shame in the sloblands of Tolka and the 'plage au Clontarf', smacking cradle names on her paramours, 'lads in scoutsch breeches', the surf spray on her face and 'the saywint up [her] ambushure'. From the city, she graduated to the 'dinkel dale of Luggelaw' and there, under the silence of the sycamores, many are allowed to roam in her kirkeyaard, including a heremite named Michael Arklow, who plies 'his newly anointed hands' into the 'strumans' of that fabled hair. To give some idea of Joyce's exigent method of writing, that same hair, which was borrowed from the head of Livia Schmitz, wife of Italo Svevo, also resembles the Dartry Reservoir, streaked red from the canisters thrown in from the nearby dye works, and Joyce being Joyce, it transforms and ends up being the colour of bog land at sundown.

Anna sets her cap at Bygmester Finnegan, a 'duddurty devil', rumoured to have committed some fiendish sexual act in the Phoenix Park. She despatches her boudeloire ninnies and backwater sals to call on Finnegan, in residence on a barge in Howth. She warns them to go 'aisy-oisy', letting on that she doesn't care. In time, Finnegan takes her as wife, having chosen her for her seven hues. Joyce's rapturous description of Anna's bridal preparations belong easily in Song of Songs:

First she let her hair fall and down it flussed to her feet its teviots winding coils. Then, mother-naked, she sampood herself with galawater and fraguant pistania mud, wupper and lauar, from crown to sole. Next she greased the groove of her keel, warthes and wears and mole and itcher, with antifouling butterscatch and turfentide and serpenthyme and with leafmould she ushered round prunella isles and islets dun quincecunct allover her little mary. Peeld gold of waxwork her jellybelly and her grains of incense anguille bronze. And after that she wove a garland for her hair. She pleated it. She plaited it. Of meadowgrass and riverflags, the bulrush and waterweed, and of fallen griefs of weeping willow. Then she made her bracelets and her anklets and her armlets and a jetty amulet for necklace of clicking cobbles and pattering pebbles and rumbledown rubble, richmond and rehr, of Irish rhunerhinerstones and shell-marble bangles. That done, a dawk of smut to her airy ey.

Anna is more Celtic geisha than traditional wife. In the 'way of a maid with a man' she tickles his pontiff's fancy with tricks and ruses, doing a turn on the fiddle, legging a jig, singing a hymn or warbling 'The Rakes of Mallow'. Her cooking comprises 'blooms of fisk' and 'staynish beacons on toast', with wishy-washy tea, 'Kaffue mokau' or fern ale in 'trueart pewter mug'. Anything to plaise him. She procures all the nice little whores, the lizzies and the doxies, 'to hug and hab haven in Humpy's apron', while wishing she did not have to. She gives birth to three children, Shem and Shaun and Izzy, named after Chapelizod who pines for her Tristan. In time, the father's affections veer towards the daughter and Anna wishes that he would rush upon her darkly, as he used, 'like a great black shadow'.

So how, for readers, does Anna Livia fulfil our notion of heroine? Is she a kindred spirit? Do we identify with her? The answer is no, not in the same way as we do with that other Anna, or Emma Bovary, or Clarissa, or Moll Flanders. She is at once too rarefied and too remote. Whereas Molly Bloom was all flesh and appetite, Anna is all essence. We do not get inside her mind or know the registers of her disenchantments as she passes from youth to age, except for a rare and piercing lamentation – 'Is there one who understands me?' Probably not, with the exception of James Joyce. Anna is the signature of Joyce in his last lonely and embattled months, a mounting phalanx of hostility towards *Finnegans Wake*; a daughter, Lucia, his in-spiritrice, committed to an asylum; walking in the snow in Zurich with his little grandson, his eyes hidden with thick, dark glasses, entrenched in that same darkness that he had, in high-hearted youth, pitied in his hero Ibsen. It was January 1941, Europe in the throes of war and Joyce, 'his heart's adrone', unknowingly on the brink of death.

Andre Gide, who had demeaned Joyce in his lifetime, ten years after Joyce's death wrote in homage that 'the greatest audacity is that at the end of life', by which he must surely have meant *Finnegan's Wake* and *Anna Livia Plurabelle*. Despite her trepidation, Anna meets her fate resolutely, as she goes towards her end, her 'cold mad feary father', the enveloping sea. 'Can't hear with bawk of bats, all the liffeying waters of. Ho, talk save us! My foos won't moos. I feel as old as yonder elm. [. . .] Who were Shem and Shaun the living sons or daughters of? Night now! [. . .] Night night! [. . .] Beside the rivering waters of, hitherandthithering waters of. Night!'

Anna is his last creation, his farewell to words, haunting, ineffable, a mythic Eve, haloed in 'the dusk of wonder'.

Edna O'Brien
September 2016

A Note on the Publishing History

Although only an early extract from the work that became *Finnegans Wake* (1939), James Joyce's *Anna Livia Plurabelle*, first published by Faber & Faber in 1930, has developed an enduring appeal in its own right. As T. S. Eliot later explained, 'This fantasy of the course of the river Liffey is the best-known part of *Finnegans Wake*, and is the best introduction to it.'

At a time when *Ulysses*, Joyce's complex and controversial masterpiece, was still proscribed in Britain, Eliot, a director of Faber & Faber, went to great pains to nurture the Irish writer's literary greatness. This included not only publishing in 1930 an authoritative guide to *Ulysses*, written by Stuart Gilbert under Joyce's own supervision; but also several extracts from Joyce's long-gestated 'Work in Progress' (as *Finnegans Wake* was then called). *Anna Livia Plurabelle* was the first of these, going on sale (price 1 shilling) in June 1930 as pamphlet no. 15 in Faber's Criterion Miscellany series. It was an immediate publishing success: by

1932 over six thousand copies had been sold and it had gone through four impressions.

Sales may have been helped by the issue of a gramophone recording by C. K. Ogden of Joyce reading a key part of *Anna Livia Plurabelle*. Listening to it, T. S. Eliot noted that 'the author's voice reciting it revealed at once a beauty which is disclosed only gradually by the printed page'. As this recording is now widely available on the Internet, readers can experience this for themselves.

The text of *Anna Livia Plurabelle* is reprinted unchanged from the 1930 Criterion Miscellany edition. When Joyce came to incorporate this episode of 'Work in Progress' in *Finnegans Wake*, he made further changes and additions to this Faber text.

Robert Brown,
Archivist, Faber & Faber
September 2016

ANNA LIVIA PLURABELLE

O

tell me all about
Anna Livia! I want to hear all
about Anna Livia. Well, you know Anna Livia?
Yes, of course, we all know Anna Livia. Tell me all.
Tell me now. You'll die when you hear. Well, you
know, when the old cheb went futt and did what
you know. Yes, I know, go on. Wash quit and don't
be dabbling. Tuck up your sleeves and loosen your
talk-tapes. And don't butt me – hike! – when you
bend. Or whatever it was they threed to make out
he thried to two in the Fiendish park. He's an awful
old reppe. Look at the shirt of him! Look at the
dirt of it! He has all my water black on me. And it
steeping and stuping since this time last wik. How
many goes is it I wonder I washed it? I know by
heart the places he likes to saale, duddurty devil!
Scorching my hand and starving my famine to
make his private linen public. Wallop it well with
your battle and clean it. My wrists are rwusty rubbing the mouldaw stains. And the dneepers of wet

and the gangres of sin in it! What was it he did a
tail at all on Animal Sendai? And how long was he
under loch and neagh? It was put in the newses
what he did, nicies and priers, the King fierceas
Humphrey, with illysus distilling, exploits and all.
But toms will till. I know he well. Temp untamed
will hist for no man. As you spring so shall you
neap. O, the roughty old rappe! Minxing marrage
and making loof. Reeve Gootch was right and
Reeve Drughad was sinistrous! And the cut of him!
And the strut of him! How he used to hold his head
as high as a howeth, the famous eld duke alien,
with a hump of grandeur on him like a walking rat.
And his derry's own drawl and his corks-own
blather and his doubling stutter and his gull-away
swank. Ask Lictor Hackett or Lector Reade or
Garda Growley or the Boy with the Billyclub. How
elster is he a called at all. Qu'appelle? Huges Caput
Earlyfouler? Or where was he born or how was he
found? Urgothland, Tvistown on the Kattekat?
New Hunshire, Concord on the Merrimake? Was
her banns never loosened in Adam and Eve's or
were him and her but captain spliced? For mine
ether duck I thee drake. And by my wildgaze I thee
gander. Flowey and Mount on the brink of time
makes wishes and fears for a happy isthmass. O,
passmore that and oxus another. Don Dom Domb-

4

domb and his wee follyo! Was his help inshored in the Stork and Pelican against bungelars, flu and third risk parties? I heard he dug good tin with his doll when he raped her home, Sabrine asthore, in a parakeet's cage, by dredgerous lands and devious delts, playing catched and mythed with the gleam of her shadda, past auld min's manse, and Maisons Allfou and the rest of incurables and the last of immurables, the quaggy waag for stumbling. Who sold you that jackalantern's tale? Pemmican's pasty pie! In a gabbard he barqued it, the boat of life, from the harbourless Ivernikan Okean, till he spied the loom of his landfall and he loosed two croakers from under his tilt, the gran Phenician rover. By the smell of her kelp they made the pigeonhouse. Like fun they did! But where was Himself, the timoneer? That marchantman he suivied their scutties right over the wash, his cameleer's burnous breezing up on him, till with his runagate bowmpriss he roade and borst her bar. Pilcomayo! Suchcaughtawan! And the whale's away with the grayling! Tune your pipes and fall ahumming, you born ijypt, and you're nothing short of one! Well, ptellomey soon and curb your escumo. When they saw him shoot swift up her sheba sheath, like any gay lord salomon, her bulls they were ruhring, surfed with spree. Boyarka buah! Boyana bueh! He erned his

5

lille Bunbath hard, our staly bred, the trader. He did. Look at here. In this wet of his prow. Don't you know he was kalled a bairn of the brine, Wasserbourne the waterbaby? Havemmarea, so he was. H.C.E. has a codfisck ee. Shyr she's nearly as badher as him herself. Who? Anna Livia? Ay, Anna Livia. Do you know she was calling backwater sals from all around to go in till him, her erring cheef, and tickle the pontiff aisy-oisy? She was? Gota pot! Well, that's the limmat! As El Negro winced when he wonced in La Plate. O, tell me all I want to hear, how loft she was lift a laddery dextro. A coneywink after the bunting fell. Letting on she didn't care, the proxenete! Proxenete and phwhat is phthat? Tell us in franca langua. And call a spate a spate. Did they never sharee you ebro at skol, you antiabecedarian? It's just the same as if I was to go for examplum now out of telekinesis and proxenete you. For coxyt sake and is that what she is? Botlettle I thought she'd act that loa. Didn't you spot her in her windaug, wubbling up on an osiery chair, with a meusic before her all cunniform letters, pretending to ribble a reedy derg on a fiddle she bogans without a band on? Sure she can't fiddan a dee, with bow or abandon! Sure, she can't! Tista suck. Well, I never heard the like of that! Tell me moher. Tell me moatst. Well, old Humber was as glommen

6

as grampus, with the tares at his thor and the buboes for ages and neither bowman nor shot abroad and bales allbrant on the crests of rockies and nera lamp in kitchen or church and giant's holes in Grafton's causeway, sittang sambre on his benk, drammen and drommen, his childlinen scarf to encourage his obsequies where he'd check their debths in that mormon's thames, be questing and handset, hop, step and a deepend, with his berths in their toiling moil, his swallower open from swolf to fore and the snipes of the gutter pecking his crocs, hungerstriking all alone and holding doomsdag over hunselv, dreeing his weird, with his dander up, and his fringe combed over his eygs and droming on loft till the sight of the sternes, after zwarthy kowse and weedy broeks and the tits of buddy and the loits of pest and to peer was Parish worth thette mess. You'd think all was dodo belonging to him how he durmed adranse in durance vaal. He had been belching for severn years. And there she was, Anna Livia, she darent catch a winkle of sleep, purling around like a chit of a child, in a Lapsummer skirt and damazon cheeks, for to ishim bonzour to her dear dubber Dan. With neuphraties and sault from his maggias. And an odd time she'd cook him up blooms of fisk and lay to his heartsfoot her meddery eygs and staynish beacons on toasc and a cupenhave so weeshywashy of Greenland's tay or a dzoupgan of Kaffue mokau an sable or Sikiang sukry or his ale of ferns in trueart pewter and a shinkobread for to plaise that man hog stay his stomicker till her pyrraknees shrunk to nutmeg graters and as rash as she'd russ with her peakload of vivers up on her sieve (his towering rage it swales and rieses) my hardey Hek he'd kast them frome him, with a stour of scorn, as much as to say you sow and you sozh, and if he didn't peg the platteau on her tawe, believe you me, she was safe enough. And then she'd esk to vistule a hymn, *The Heart Bowed Down* or *The Rakes of Mallow* or Chelli Michele's *La Calumnia è un Vermicelli* or a balfy bit ov *old Jo Robidson.* Sucho fuffing a fifeing 'twould cut you in two! She'd bate the hen that crowed on the turrace of Babbel. What harm if she knew how to cockle her mouth! And not a mag out of Hum no more than out of the mangle weight. Is that a faith? That's the fact. Then riding the ricka and roya romanche Annona, gebroren aroostokrat Nivia, dochter of Sense and Art, with Sparks' pirryphlickathims funkling her fan, anner frostivying tresses dasht with virevlies, – while the prom beauties sreeked nith their bearers' skins! – in a period gown of changeable jade that would robe the wood of two cardinals' chairs and crush poor Cullen and smother MacCabe. O blazerskate! Theirs porpor patches! And brahming to him down the feedchute, with all kinds of fondling endings, the poother rambling off her nose: *Vuggybarney, Wickerymandy! Hello, ducky, please don't die!* Do you know what she started cheeping then, with a choicey voicey like water-glucks? You'll never guess. Tell me. Tell me. *Phoebe, dearest, tell, O tell me* and *I loved you better nor you knew.* And letting on hoon var daft about the warbly sangs from over holmen: *High hellskirt saw ladies hensmoker lilyhung pigger:* and soay and soan and so firth and so forth in a tone sonora and Oom Bothar below in his sandy cloak, so umvolosy, as deaf as a yawn, the stult! Go away! Poor deef, old deary! Yare only teasing! Anna Liv? As chalk is my judge! And didn't she up in sorgues and go and trot doon and stand in her douro, puffing her old dudheen, and every shirvant siligirl or wensum farmerette walking the pilend roads Sawy, Fundally, Daery or Maery, Milucre, Awny or Graw, usedn't she make her a simp or sign to slip inside by the sullyport? You don't say the sillypost? I did. And do. Calling them in one by one (To Blockbeddum here! Here the Shoebenacaddie!) and legging a jig or so on the sihl to show them how to shake their benders and the dainty how to bring to mind the gladdest garments out of sight and all the way of a maid with a man and making a sort of cackling noise like two and a penny or half a crown and holding up a silliver shiner. Lordy, lordy, did she so? Well, of all the ones ever I heard! Throwing all the neiss little whores in the world at him! To inny captured wench you wish of no matter what sex of pleissful ways two adda tammar a lizzy a lossie to hug and hab haven in Humpy's apron!

And what was the wyerye rima she made! Odet! Odet! Tell me the trent of it while I'm lathering hail out of Denis Florence MacCarthy's combies. Rise it, flut ye, pian piena! I'm dying down off my iodine feet until I lerryn Anna Livia's cushingloo! I can see that, I see you are. How does it tummel? Listen now. Are you listening? Yes, yes! Idneed I am! Tarn your ore ouse. Essonne inne.

By earth and the cloudy but I badly want a brandnew bankside, bedamp and I do, and a plumper at that!

For the putty affair I have is wore out, so it is, sitting, yaping and waiting for my old Dane hodder dodderer, my life in death companion, my frugal key of our larder, my much-altered camel's hump, my jointspoiler, my maymoon's honey, my fool to the last Decemberer, to wake himself out of his winter's doze and bore me down like he used to.

Is there irwell a lord of the manor or a knight of the shire at strike, I wonder, that'd dip me a pound or two in cash for washing and darning his worshipful socks for him now we're run out of horsemeat and milk?

Only for my short Brittas bed made's as snug as it smells it's out I'd lep and off with me to the slobs della Tolka or the plage au Clontarf to feale the gay aire of my salt troublin bay and the race of the saywint up me ambushure.

Onon! Onon! tell me more. Tell me every tiny teign. I want to know every single ingul. Down to what made the potters fly into jagsthole. And why were the vesles vet. Well, now comes the hazelhatchery part. After Clondalkin the Kings's Inns. We'll soon be there with the freshet. How many aleveens had she in tool? I can't rightly rede you that. Close only knows. Some say she had three figures to fill and confined herself to a hundred eleven, wan bywan bywan. Olaph lamm et, all that pack? We won't have room in the kirkeyaard. She can't remember half of the cradlenames she smacked on them by the grace of her boxing bishop's infallible slipper, the cane for Kund and abbles for Eyolf, and ayther nayther for Yakov Yea. A hundred and how? They did well to rechristien her Pluhurabelle. O loreley! What a loddon lodes! Heigh ho! But it's quite on the cards she'll shed more and merrier, twills and trills, sparefours and spoilfives, nordsihkes and sudsevers and ayes and neins to a litter. Grandfarthring nap and Messamisery and the knave of all knaves and the joker. Heehaw! She must have been a gadabount in her day, so she must, more than most. Shoal she was, gidgad. She had a flewmen of her owen. Then a toss nare scared that lass, so aimai moe, that's agapo! Tell me, tell me, how cam she camlin through all her fellows, the neckar she was, the diveline? Linking one and knocking the next, tapting a flank and tipting a jutty and palling in and pietaring out and clyding by on her eastway. Waiwhou was the first thurever burst? Someone he was, whuebra they were, in a tactic attack or in single combat. Tinker, tilar, souldrer, salor, Pieman Peace or Polistaman. That's the thing I always want to know. Push up and push upper and come to headquarters! Was it waterlows year, after Grattan or Flood, or when maids were in Arc or when three stood hosting? Fidaris will find where the Doubt arises like Nieman from Nirgends found the Nihil. Worry you sighin foh, Albern, O Anser? Untie the gemman's fistiknots, Qvic and Nuancee? She can't put her hand on him for the moment. Tez thelon langlo, walking weary! Such a loon way backwards to row! She says herself she hardly knows whuon the annals her graveller was, a dynast of Leinster, a wolf of the sea, or what he did or how blyth she played or how, when, why, where and who offon he jumpnad her. She was just a young thin pale soft shy slim slip of a thing then, sauntering, by silvamoonlake and he was a heavy trudging lurching lieabroad of a Curraghman, making his hay for whose sun to shine on, as tough as the oaktrees (peats be with them!) used to rustle that time down by the dykes of killing Kildare, for forstfellfoss with a plash across her. She thought she's sankh neathe the ground with nymphant shame when he gave her the tigris eye! O happy fault! Me wish it was he! You're wrong there, corribly wrong! Tisn't only tonight you're anacheronistic! It was ages behind that when nullahs were nowhere, in county Wickenlow, garden of Erin, before she ever dreamt she'd lave Kilbride and go foaming under Horsepass bridge with the great southerwestern windstorming her traces and the midland's grainwaster asarch for her track, to wend her ways byandby, robecca or worse, to spin and to grind, to swab and to thrash, for all her golden lifey in the barleyfields and pennylotts of Humphrey's fordofhurdlestown and lie with a landleaper, wellingtonorseher. Alesse, the lagos of girly days! For the dove of the dunas! Wasut? Izod?

Are you sarthin suir? Not where the Finn fits into
the Mourne, not where the Nore takes lieve of
Blœm, not where the Braye divarts the Farer, not
where the Moy changez her minds twixt Cullin and
Conn tween Cunn and Collin? Neya, narev, nen
and nos! Then whereabouts in Ow and Ovoca?
Was it yst with wyst or Lucan Yokan or where the
hand of man has never set foot? Dell me where, the
fairy ferse time! I will if you listen. You know the
dinkel dale of Luggelaw? Well, there once dwelt a
local heremite, Michael Arklow was his riverend
name, (with many a sigh I aspersed his lavabibs!)
and one venersderg in juno-july, oso sweet and so
cool and so limber she looked, Nance the Nixie,
Nanon L'Escaut, in the silence, of the sycomores,
all listening, the kindling curves you simply can't
stop feeling, he plunged both of his newly anointed
hands the core of his cushlas in her singimari saf-
fron strumans of hair, parting them and soothing
her and mingling it, that was deep-dark and ample
like this red bog at sundown. By that Vale Vow-
close's lucydlac, the reignbeau's heavenarches
arronged orranged her. Afroth-dizzying galbs, her
enamelled eyes indergoading him on to the vierge
violetian. Wish a wish! Why a why? Mavro! Letty
Lerck's lafing light throw those laurals now on her
daphdaph teasesong petrock. Maass! He cuddle

not help himself, thurso that hot on him, he had to forget the monk in the man so, rubbing her up and smoothing her down, he baised his lippes in smiling mood, kiss akiss after kisokushk (as he warned her never to, never to, never) on Anna-na-Poghue's of the freckled forehead. While you'd parse secheressa she hielt her souff'. But she ruz two feet hire in her aisne aestumation. And steppes on stilts ever since. O, wasn't he the bold priest? And wasn't she the naughty Livvy? Nautic Naama's now her navn. Two lads in scoutsch breeches went through her before that, Barefoot Burn and Wallowme Wade, Lugnaquillia's noblesse pickts, before she had a hint of a hair at her fanny to hide or a bossom to tempt a birch canoedler not to mention a bulgic porterhouse barge. And ere that again, leada, laida, all unraidy, too faint to buoy the fairiest rider, too frail to flirt with a cygnet's plume, she was licked by a hound, Chirripa-Chirruta, while poing her pee, pure and simple, on the spur of the hill in old Kippure, in birdsong and shearingtime, but first of all, worst of all, the wiggly livvly, she sideslipped out by a gap in the Devil's glen while Sally her nurse was sound asleep in a sloot and feefee fiefie fell over a spillway before she found her stride and lay and wriggled in all the stagnant black pools of rainy under a fallow coo and she laughed innocefree with her limbs aloft and a whole drove of maiden hawthorns blushing and looking askance upon her.

Drop me the sound of the findhorn's name. And drip me why in the flenders was she frickled. And trickle me through was she marcellewaved or was it weirdly a wig she wore. And whitside did they droop their glows in their florry, aback to wist or affront to sea? In fear to hear the dear so near or longing loth and loathing longing? Are you in the swim or are you out? O go in, go on, go an! I mean about what you know. I know right well what you mean. Rother! You'd like the coifs and guimpes, snouty, and me to do the greasy jub on old Veronica's wipers. What am I rancing now and I'll thank you? Is it a pinny or is it a surplice? Arran, where's your nose? And where's the starch? That's not the vesdre benediction smell. I can tell from here by their *eau de Colo* and the scent of her oder they're Mrs Magrath's. And you ought to have aird them. They've moist come off her. Creases in silk they are, not crampton lawn. Baptiste me, father, for she has sinned! Through her catchment ring she freed them easy, with her hips'hurrahs for her knees'dontelleries. The only parr with frills in old the plain. So they are, I declare! Welland well! If tomorrow keeps fine who'll come tripping to sightsee?

How'll? Ask me next what I haven't got! The Belve-
darean exhibitioners. In their sculling caps and
oarsclub colours. What hoo, they band! And what
hoa, they buck! And here is her nubilee letters too.
Ellis on quay in scarlet thread. Linked for the
world on a flushcoloured field. Annan exe after to
show they're not Laura Kehoe's. O, may the dia-
bolo twisk your seifety pin! You child of Mammon,
Kinsella's Lilith! Now who has been tearing the leg
of her drawers on her? Which leg is it? The one
with the bells on it. Rinse them out and aston along
with you. Where did I stop? Never stop. Continuar-
ration! You're not there yet. Garonne, garonne!

Well, after it was put in the Mercy Cordial Men-
dicants' Sitterdag-Zindeh-Munaday Wakeschrift
(for once they sullied their white kidloves, chewing
cuds after their dinners of cheeckin and beggin,
with their show us it here and their mind out of
that and their when you're quite finished with the
reading matarial), even the snee that snowdon his
hoaring hair had a skunner against him. Thaw,
thaw, sava, savuto! Score Her Chuff Exsquire!
Everywhere erriff you went and every bung you
arver dropped into, in cit or suburb or in addled
areas, the Rose and Bottle or Phoenix Tavern or
Power's Inn or Jude's Hotel, or wherever you
scoured the countryside from Nannywater to Var-

tryville or from Porta Lateen to the lootin quarter
you found his ikom etsched tipside down or the
cornerboys burning his guy and Morris the Man,
with the role of a royss in his turgos the turrible,
(Evropeahahn cheic house, unskimmed sooit and
yahoort, hamman now cheekmee, Ahdahm this
way make, Fatima, half turn!) reeling and railing
round the local with oddfellow's triple tiara busby
rotundarinking round his scalp. Like Pate-by-the-
Neva or Pete-over-Meer. This is the Hausman all
paven and stoned, that cribbed the Cabin that
never was owned, that cocked his leg and hennad
his Egg. And the mauldrin rabble around him in
areopage, fracassing a great bingkan cagnan with
their timpan crowders. Mind your Grimmfather!
Think of your Ma! Hing the Hong is his jove's
hangnomen! Lilt a bolero, bulling a law! She swore
on croststyx nyne wyndabouts she'd be level with
all the snags of them yet. Par the Vulnerable Vir-
gin's Mary del Dame! So she said to herself she'd
frame a plan to fake a shine, the mischiefmaker, the
like of it you niever heard. What plan? Tell me
quick and dongu so crould! What the meurther did
she mague? Well, she bergened a bag, a shammy
mailbag, off one of her swapsons, Shaun the Post,
and then she went and consulted her chapboucqs,
old Mot Moore, Casey's Euclid and the Fashion

Display and made herself tidal to join in the mascarete. O gig goggle of gigguels. I can't tell you how! It's too screaming to rizo, rabbit it all! Minneha, minnehi minaaehe, minneho! O but you must, you must really. Make my hear it gurgle gurgle, like the farest gargle gargle in the dusky dirgle dargle. By the holy well of Mulhuddart I swear I'd pledge my chanza getting to heaven through Terry and Killy's mount of impiety to hear it all, aviary word. O, leave me my faculties, woman, a while. If you don't like my story get out of the punt. Well, have it your own way, so. Here, sit down and do as you're bid. Take my stroke and bend to your bow. Forward in and pull your overthepoise! Lisp it slaney and crisp it quiet. Deel me longsome. Tongue your time now. Breathe thet deep. Thouat's the fairway. Hurry slow and scheldt you go. Lynd us your blessed ashes here till I scrub the canon's underpants. Flow now. Ower more.

First she let her hair fall and down it flussed to her feet its teviots winding coils. Then, mothernaked, she sampood herself with galawater and fraguant pistania mud, wupper and lauar, from crown to sole. Next she greased the groove of her keel, warthes and wears and mole and itcher, with antifouling butterscatch and turfentide and serpenthyme and with leafmould she ushered round prunella isles and islets dun quincecunct allover her little mary. Peeld gold of waxwork her jellybelly and her grains of incense anguille bronze. And after that she wove a garland for her hair. She pleated it. She plaited it. Of meadowgrass and riverflags, the bulrush and waterweed, and of fallen griefs of weeping willow. Then she made her bracelets and her anklets and her armlets and a jetty amulet for necklace of clicking cobbles and pattering pebbles and rumbledown rubble, richmond and rehr, of Irish rhunerhinerstones and shell-marble bangles. That done, a dawk of smut to her airy ey, Annushka Lutetiavitch Pufflovah, and the lellipos cream to her lippeleens and the pick of the paintbox for her pommettes, from strawbirry reds to extra violates, and she sent her boudeloire maids to His Affluence, Ciliegia Grande and Kirschie Real, the two chirsines, with respecks from his missus, seepy and sewery, and a request might she passe of him for a minnikin. A call to pay, and light a taper, in Brie-on-Arrosa, back in sprizzling. The cock striking mine, the stalls bridely sign, there's Zambosy waiting for me. She said she wouldn't be half her length away. Then, then, as soon as the lump his back was turned, with her mealiebag slang over her shulder, Anna Livia, oysterface, forth of her bassein came.

Describe her! Hustle along, why can't you? Spitz on the iern while it's hot. I wouldn't miss her for irthing on nerthe. Oceans of Gaud, I mussel hear that! Ogowe presta! Leste, before Julia sees her! Ishekarry and washemeskad, the carishy caratimaney? Whole lady fair? Duodecimoroon? Bon a ventura? Malagassy? What had she on, the liddel oud oddity? How much did she scallop, harness and weights? Here she is, Amnisty Ann! Call her calamity electrifies man.

No electress at all, but old Moppa Necessity, angin mother of injons. I'll tell you a test. But you must sit still. Will you hold your peace and listen well to what I am going to say now? It might have been ten or twenty to one of the night of Allclose or the nexth of April when the flip of her hoogly igloo flappered and out toetippit a bushman woman, the dearest little moma ever you saw, nodding around her, all smiles, with ems of embarras and aues to awe, between two ages, a judyqueen, not up to your elb. Quick, look at her cute and saise her quirk for the bicker she lives the slicker she grows. Save us and tagus! No more? Werra where in ourthe did you ever pick a Lambay chop as big as a battering ram? Ay, you're right. I'm epte to forgetting, Like Liviam Liddle did Loveme Long. The linth of my hough, I say! She wore a ploughboy's nailstudded clogs, a pair of ploughfields in themselves: a sugarloaf hat with a gaudyquiviry peak and a band of gorse for an arnoment and a hundred streamers dancing off it and a guildered pin to pierce it: owlglassy bicycles boggled her eyes: and a fishnetzeveil she had to keep the sun from spoiling her wrinkles: potatorings boucled the loose laubes of her laudsnarers: her nude cuba stockings were salmospotspeckled: she sported a galligo shimmy of hazevaipar tinto that never was fast till it ran in the washing: stout stays, the rivals, lined her length: her bloodorange bockknickers, a two in one garment, showed natural nigger boggers, fancyfastened, free to undo: her blackstripe tan joseph was sequansewn and teddybearlined, with wavy rushgreen epaulettes and a leadown here and there of royal swansruff: a brace of gaspers stuck in her hayrope garters: her civvy codroy coat with alpheubett buttons was boundaried round with a twobar tunnel belt: a fourpenny bit in each pocketside weighed her safe from the blowaway windrush; she had a clothespeg tight astride on her joki's nose and she kep on grinding a sommething quaint in her fiumy mouth and the rrreke of the fluve of the tail of the gawan of her snuffdrab siouler's skirt trailed ffiffty Irish miles behind her lungarhodes.

Hellsbells, I'm sorry I missed her! Sweet gumptyum and nobody fainted. But in whelk of her mouths? Was her naze alight? Everyone that saw her said the dowce little delia looked a bit queer. Lotsy trotsy, mind the poddle! Missus, be good and don't fol in the say! Fenny poor hex she must have charred. Kickhams a frumpier ever you saw. Making saft mullet's eyes at her boys dobelong. And they crowned her their chariton queen, all the maids. Of the may? You don't say! Well for her she couldn't see herself. I recknitz wharfore the darling murrayed her mirror. She did? Mersey me! There was a koros of drouthdropping surfacemen, boomslanging and plugchewing, fruiteyeing and flowerfeeding, in contemplation of the fluctuation and the undification of her filimentation, lolling and leasing on North Lazers' Waal all eelfare week by the Jukar Yoick's and as soon as they saw her meander by that marritime way in her grasswinter's weeds and twigged who was under her deaconess bonnet, Avondale's fish and Clarence's poison, says an to aneber, Wit-upon-Crutches to Master Bates: *Between our two southsates and the granite they're warming, or her face has been lifted or Alp has doped.*

But what was the game in her mixed baggyrhatty? And where in thunder did she plunder?

Fore the battle or efter the ball? I want to get it frisk from the soorce. I aubette my bearb it's worth while poaching on. Shake it up, do, do! That's a good old son of a ditch! I promise. I'll make it worth your while. And I don't mean maybe. Not yet with a goodfor. Spey me pruth and I'll tale you true.

Well, arundgirond in a waveney lyne aringa-rouma she pattered and swung and sidled, dribbling her boulder through narrowa mosses, the dilisky-drear on our drier side and the vilde vetchvine agin us, curara here careero there, not knowing which medway or weser to strike it, edereider making chattahoochee all to her ain chichiu, like Santa Claus at the cree of the pale and puny, nistling to hear for their tiny hearties, her arms encircling Iso-labella, then running with reconciled Romas and Reims, then bathing Dirty Hans' spatters with spit-tle, with a Christmas box apiece for aisch and ivery-one of her childer, the birthday gifts they dreamt they gabe her, the spoiled she fleetly laid at our door! On the matt, by the pourch and inunder the cellar. The rivulets ran aflod to see, the glashaboys, the pollynooties. Out of the paunschaup on to the pyre. And they all about her, youths and maidens, rickets and riots, like the Smyly boys at their vice-reine's levee. Vivi vienne, little Annchen vielo Anna,

high life! Sing us a sula, O, susuria! Ausone sidul-
cis! Hasn't she tambre! Chipping her and raising a
bit of a chir or a jary every dive she'd neb in her
culdee sacco of wabbash she raabed and reach out
her maundy meerschaundize, poor souvenir as per
ricorder and all for sore aringarung, stinkers and
heelers, laggards and primelads, her furzeborn sons
and dribblederry daughters, a thousand and one of
them, and wickerpotluck for each of them. For evil
and ever. And kiks the buch. A tinker's bann and a
barrow to boil his billy for Gipsy Lee; a cartridge
of cockaleekie soup for Chummy the Guardsman;
for sulky Pender's acid nephew deltoïd drops, cur-
iously strong; a cough and a rattle and wildrose
cheeks for poor Piccolina Petite MacFarlane; a jig-
saw puzzle of needles and pins and blankets and
shins between them for Isabel, Jezebel and Llewe-
lyn Mmarriage; a brazen nose and pigiron mittens
for Johnny Walker Beg; a papar flag of the saints
and stripes for Kevineen O'Dea; a puffpuff for
Pudge Craig and a nightmarching hare for Techer
Tombigby; waterleg and gumboots each for Bully
Hayes and Hurricane Hartigan; a prodigal heart
and fatted calves for Buck Jones, the pride of Clon-
liffe; a loaf of bread and a father's early aim for
Tim from Skibereen; a jauntingcar for Larry Doo-
lin, the Ballyclee jackeen; a seasick trip on a gov-

ernment ship for Teague O'Flanagan; a louse and
trap for Jerry Coyle; slushmincepies for Andy
Mackenzie; a hairclip and clackdish for Penceless
Peter; that twelve sounds look for G. V. Brooke; a
drowned doll, to face downwards for modest Sister
Anne Mortimer; altar falls for Blanchisse's bed;
Wildairs' breeketties for Magpeg Woppington; to
Sue Dot a big eye, to Sam Dash a false step; snakes
in clover, picked and scotched and a vaticanned
viper-catcher's visa for Patsy Presbys; a reiz every
morning for Standfast Dick and a drop every min-
ute for Stumblestone Davy; scruboak beads for
beatified Biddy; two appletweed stools for Eva
Mobbely; for Saara Philpot a jordan vale tearorne;
a pretty box of Pettyfib's Powder for Eileen Aruna
to whiten her teeth and outflash Helen Arhone; a
whippingtop for Eddy Lawless; for Kitty Coleraine
of Butterman's Lane a penny wise for her foolish
pitcher; a putty shovel for Terry the Puckaun; a
apotamus mask for Promoter Dunne; a niester egg
with a twicedated shell and a dynamight right for
Pavl the Curate; a collera morbous for Mann in the
Cloack; a starr and girton for Draper and Deane;
for Will-of-the-Wisp and Barny the Bark two man-
golds noble to sweeden their bitters; for Oliver
Bound a way in his frey; for Seumas, thought little,
a crown he feels big; a tibertine's pile with a Con-

goswood cross on the back for Sunny Twimjim; a
praises be and spare me days for Brian the Bravo;
penteplenty of pity with lubilashings of lust for
Olona Lena Magdalena; for Camilla, Dromilla,
Ludmilla, Mamilla, a bucket, a packet, a book and
a pillow; for Nancy Shannon a Tuami brooch; for
Dora Riparia Hopeandwater a cooling douche and
a warmingpan; a pair of Blarney braggs for Wally
Meagher; a hairpin slatepencil for Elsie Oram to
scratch her toby, doing her best with her volgar
fractions; an old age pension for Betty Bellezza; a
bag of the blues for Funny Fitz; a *Missa pro Messa*
for Taff de Taff; Jill, the spoon of a girl, for Jack,
the broth of a boy; a Rogerson Crusoe's Friday fast
for Caducus Angelus Rubiconstein; three hundred
and sixtysix poplin tyne for revery warp in the
weaver's woof for Victor Hugonot; a stiff steaded
rake and good varians muck for Kate the Cleaner;
a hole in the ballad for Hosty; two dozen of cradles
for J. F. X. P. Coppinger; tenpounten on the pop for
the daulphins born with five spoiled squibs for
Infanta; a letter to last a lifetime for Maggi beyond
by the ashpit; the heftiest frozenmeat woman from
Lusk to Livienbad for Felim the Ferry; spas and
speranza and symposium's syrup for decayed and
blind and gouty Gough; a change of naves and joys
of ills for Armoricus Tristram Amoor Saint Law-

rence; a guillotine shirt for Reuben Redbreast und hempen suspendeats for Brennan on the Moor; an oakanknee for Conditor Sawyer and musquodoboits for Great Tropical Scott; a C3 peduncle for Karmalite Kane; a sunless map of the month, including the sword and stamps for Shemus O'Shaun the Post; a jackal with hide for Browne but Nolan; a stonecold shoulder for Donn Joe Vance; all lock and no stable for Honorbright Meretrix; a big drum for Billy Dunboyne; a guilty goldeny bellows, below me blow me for Ida Ida and a hushaby rocker Elletrouvetout for Who-is-silvier – Where-is-he?; whatever you like to swilly to swash Yuinness or Yennessy, Laagen or Niger, for Festus King and Roaring Peter and Frisky Shorty and Treacle Tom and O. B. Behan and Sully the Thug and Master Magrath and Peter Cloran and O'Delawarr Rossa and Nerone MacPacem and whoever you chance to meet knocking around; and a pig's bladder balloon for Selina Susquehanna Stakelum. But what did she give to Pruda Ward and Katty Kanel and Peggy Quilty and Briery Brosna and Teasy Kieran and Ena Lappin and Muriel Mosel and Zusan Camac and Melissa Bradogue and Flora Ferns and Fauna Fox-Goodman and Grettna Greaney and Penelope Inglesante and Lezba Licking like Leytha Liane and Roxana Rohan

with Simpatica Sohan and Una Bina Laterza and
Trina La Mesme and Philomena O'Farrell and
Irmak Elly and Josephine Foyle and Snakeshead
Lily and Fountainoy Laura and Marie Xavier Agnes
Daisy Frances de Sales Macleay? She gave them
ilcka madre's daughter a moonflower and a blood-
vein: but the grapes that ripe before reason to them
that devide the vinedress. So on Izzy, her shame-
maid, love shone befond her tears as from Shem, her
penmight, life past befoul his prime.

My colonial, wardha bagful! A bakereen's
dusind with tithe tillies to boot. That's what you
may call a tale of a tub. All that and more under
one crinoline envelope if you dare to break the
porkbarrel seal. No wonder they'd run from her
pison plague. Throw us your hudson soap for the
honour of Clane. The wee taste the water left. I'll
raft it back, first thing in the marne. Merced
mulde! Ay, and don't forget the reckitts I lohaned
you. You've all the swirls your side of the current.
Well, am I to blame for that if I have! Who said
you're to blame for that if you have? You're a bit
on the sharp side. I'm on the wide. Only snuffers'
cornets drifts my way that the cracka dvine chucks
out of his cassock, with her estheryear's marsh nar-
cissus to make him recant his vanitty fair. Foul
strips of his chinook's bible I do be reading, dod-

well disgustered but chickled with chuckles at the tittles is drawn on the tattle-page. *Senior ga dito: Faciasi Omo! E omo fu fò.* Ho! Ho! *Senior ga dito: Faciasi Hidamo! Hidamo se ga facessà.* Ha! Ha! And *Die Windermere Dichter* and Lefanu (Sheridan's) *Old House by the Coachyard* and Mill (J.) *On Woman* with *Ditto on the Floss.* Ja, a swamp for Altmuehler and a stone for his flossies. I know how racy they move his wheel. My hands are blawcauld between isker and suda like that piece of pattern chayney there, lying below. Or where is it? Lying beside the sedge I saw it. Hoangho, my sorrow, I've lost it! Aimihi! With that turbary water who could see? So near and yet so far! But O, gihon! I lovat a gabber. I could listen to maure and moravar again. Regn onder river. Flies do your float. Thick is the life for mere.

Well, you know or don't you kennet or haven't I told you every telling has a taling and that's the he and the she of it. Look, look, the dusk is growing. My branches lofty are taking root. And my cold cher's gone ashley. Fieluhr? Filou! What age is at? It saon is late. 'Tis endless now since eye or erewone last saw Waterhouse's clogh. They took it asunder, I hurd thum sigh. When will they reassemble it? O, my back, my back, my bach! I'd want to go to Aches-les-Pains. Pingpong! There's the Belle

30

for Sexaloitez! And Concepta de Send-us-pray!
Pang! Wring out the clothes! Wring in the dew!
Godavari, vert the showers! And grant thaya grace!
Aman. Will we spread them here now? Ay, we will.
Flip! Spread on your bank and I'll spread mine on
mine. Flep! It's what I'm doing. Spread! It's churn-
ing chill. Der went is rising. I'll lay a few stones on
the hostel sheets. A man and his bride embraced
between them. Else I'd have sprinkled and folded
them only. And I'll tie my butcher's apron here. It's
suety yet. The strollers will pass it by. Six shifts, ten
kerchiefs, nine to hold to the fire and this for the
code, the convent napkins twelve, one baby's
shawl. Good mother Jossiph knows, she said.
Whose head? Mutter snores? Deataceas! Wharnow
are alle her childer, say? In kingdome gone or
power to come or gloria be to them farther? Alla-
livial, allalluvial! Some here, more no more, more
again lost alla stranger. I've heard tell that same
brooch of the Shannons was married into a family
in Spain. And all the Dunders de Dunnes in Mark-
land's Vineland beyond Brendan's herring pool
takes number nine in yangsee's hats. And one of
Biddy's beads went bobbing till she rounded up lost
histereve with a marigold and a cobbler's candle in
a side strain of a main drain of a manzinahurries
off Bachelor's Walk. But all that's left to the last of

the Meaghers in the loup of the years prefixed and
between is one knee-buckle and two hooks in the
front. Do you tell me that now? I do in troth.
Orara por Orbe and poor Las Animas! Ussa, Ulla,
we're umbas all! Mezha, didn't you hear it a deluge
of times, ufer and ufer, respund to spond? You
deed, you deed! I need, I need! It's that irrawad-
dyng I've stoke in my aars. It all but husheth the
lethest sound. Oronoko! What's your trouble? Is
that the great Finnleader himself in his joakimono
on his statue riding the high horse there forehen-
gist? Father of Otters, it is himself! Yonne there!
Isset that? On Fallareen Common? You're thinking
of Astley's Amphitheayter where the bobby
restrained you making sugarstuck pouts to the
ghost-white horse of the Peppers. Throw the cob-
webs from your eyes, woman, and spread your
washing proper. It's well I know your sort of slop.
Flap! Ireland sober is Ireland stiff. Lord help you,
Maria, full of grease, the load is with me! Your
prayers. I sonht zo! Madammangut! Were you lift-
ing your elbow, tell us, glazy cheeks, in Conway's
Carrigacurra canteen? Was I what, hobbledyhips?
Flop! Your rere gait's creakorheuman bitts your
butts disagrees. Amn't I up since the damp dawn,
marthared mary allacook, with Corrigan's pulse
and varicoarse veins, my pram-axle smashed, Alice

Jane in decline and my oneeyed mongrel twice run over, soaking and bleaching boiler rags, and sweating cold, a widow like me, for to deck my tennis champion son, the laundryman with the lavender flannels? You won your limpopo limp fron the husky hussars when Collars and Cuffs was heir to the town and your slur gave the stink to Carlow. Holy Scamander, I sar it again! Near the golden falls. Icis on us! Seints of light! Zezere! Subdue your noise, you hamble creature! What is it but a blackburry growth or the dwyergray ass them four old codgers owns. Are you meanam Tarpey and Lyons and Gregory? I meyne now, thank all, the four of them, and the roar of them, that draves that stray in the mist and old Johnny MacDougal along with them. Is that the Poolbeg flasher beyant, pharphar, or a fireboat coasting nyar the Kishtna or a glow I behold within a hedge or my Garry come back from the Indes? Wait till the honeying of the lune, love! Die eve, little eve, die! We see that wonder in your eye. We'll meet again, we'll part once more. The spot I'll seek if the hour you'll find. My chart shines high where the blue milk's upset. Forgivemequick, I'm going! Bubye! And you, pluck your watch, forgetmenot. Your evenlode. So save to jurna's end! My sights are swimming thicker on me by the shadows to this place. I sow home slowly

now by own way, moyvalley way. Towy I too, rath-
mine.

Ah, but she was the queer old skeowsha anyhow,
Anna Livia, trinkettoes. And sure he was the quare
old buntz too, Dear Dirty Dumpling, foosther-
father of fingalls and dotthergills. Gammer and gaf-
fer we're all their gangsters. Hadn't he seven dams
to wive him? And every dam had her seven
crutches. And every crutch had its seven hues. And
each hue had a differing cry. Sudds for me and sup-
per for you and the doctor's bill for Joe John.
Befor! Bifur! He married his markets, cheap by
foul, I know, like any Etrurian Catholic Heathen,
in their pinky limony creamy birnies and their tur-
kiss indienne mauves. But at milkidmass who was
the spouse? Then all that was was fair. Tys Elven-
land? Teems of times and happy returns. The seim
anew. Ordovico or viricordo. Anna was, Livia is,
Plurabelle's to be. Northmen's thing made south-
folk's place but howmulty plurators made eachone
in person? Latin me that, my trinity scholard, out
of eure sanscreed into oure eryan. *Hircus Civis
Eblanensis!* He had buckgoat paps on him, soft
ones for orphans. Ho, Lord! Twins of his bosom.
Lord save us! And ho! Hey? What all men. Hot?
His tittering daughters of. Whawk?

Can't hear with the waters of. The chittering
34

waters of. Flittering bats, fieldmice bawk talk. Ho! Are you not gone ahome? What Tom Malone? Can't hear with bawk of bats, all the liffeying waters of. Ho, talk save us! My foos won't moos. I feel as old as yonder elm. A tale told of Shaun or Shem? All Livia's daughtersons. Dark hawks hear us. Night! Night! My ho head halls. I feel as heavy as yonder stone. Tell me of John or Shaun? Who were Shem and Shaun the living sons or daughters of? Night now! Tell me, tell me, tell me, elm! Night night! Telmetale of stem or stone. Beside the rivering waters of, hitherandthithering waters of. Night!

Faber Modern Classics was launched in April 2015, and draws upon Faber & Faber's unique and diverse publishing since the company was first established in 1929. With titles from the fiction, non-fiction, poetry and drama lists brought together in one beautiful livery, these are the books and authors who have earned Faber a reputation for publishing the most powerful and original writing of each generation.

Faber & Faber is one of the great independent publishing houses. We were established in 1929 by Geoffrey Faber, with T. S. Eliot as one of our first editors. We are proud to publish award-winning fiction and non-fiction, as well as an unrivalled list of poets and playwrights. Among our writers we have five Booker Prize-winners and twelve Nobel Laureates, and we continue to seek out the most exciting and innovative writers at work today.